Clifford's
Field Day

Norman Bridwell

Cartwheel
·B·O·O·K·S· ®

SCHOLASTIC INC.
New York   Toronto   London   Auckland
Sydney   Mexico City   New Delhi   Hong Kong

For Jennifer Naomi Morris

The author thanks Manny Campana and Grace Maccarone for their contributions to this book.

ISBN 978-0-545-22325-6

10 9 8 7 6 5 4 3 2   12 13 14 15 16/0

Printed in the U.S.A.   40
First printing, March 1996
This edition printing, February 2012

Clifford is excited for Field Day.

There will be games.
There will be races.

The sack race is first.

Clifford is so big, he needs four sacks.

Coach says Clifford needs to use one sack.
Emily Elizabeth gets him a bigger one.

Then the sack race starts.

Oops! Clifford falls down.

The three-legged race is about to start.

Clifford is better at that.

Now Clifford wants to try
jumping over the hurdles.

He wants to jump over three
hurdles at one time.

Uh-oh! The hurdles are not
so easy after all.

Tumbling is next.

Way to go, Clifford!

Clifford is very good at tumbling.

Clifford is the best.

He gets a perfect 10!

Now it is time for a tug-of-war.

Emily Elizabeth and her team need help.

Clifford joins Emily Elizabeth's team.

They win!

The coach says, "That's not fair.
Clifford is too big to play."

Clifford is sad. He just wants to
have fun with the boys and girls.

Finally, it is time for the ball game.

Clifford just sits and watches.

The batter hits the ball far, far away.
Clifford can help.

Oh no! A boy is running in front of a car!

Clifford stops him just in time.

The boy is safe.

Clifford is the hero of the day!